"If you live in the local area like I do, keep your curtains drawn and keep your lamps on high before you read this book.

Highly strange cases that kept me up and questioning what's out there right in my backyard!

If you love local accounts of paranormal activity direct from a consummate investigator like Eric Mintel, this is it.
Compelling!!
5 stars plus!!"

Anna Maria Manalo
Author "Haunted Heirlooms"

ERIC MINTEL INVESTIGATES
CASEBOOK INVESTIGATIONS 2016-STORIES, ENCOUNTERS AND OTHERWORLDLY CONTACT.

BY
ERIC MINTEL

EMI Press
Printed in the USA

The author has recreated events as they happened on each individual case.

First Printing July 2024

Volume One

© 2024 by Eric Mintel

ericmintelinvestigates.org Subscribe to the Eric Mintel Investigates You Tube Channel.

Eric Mintel Investigates: Casebook Files 2016-Stories, encounters and otherworldly contact!

I've been fascinated by the paranormal since childhood. Ghost stories, phantoms, and apparitions filled my early years, often recounted by my father based on his own encounters. Living in Bucks County, PA, where there's a rich history of paranormal activity—ranging from ghosts and Bigfoot to UFOs and more—only fueled my curiosity.

Throughout most of my life, I've pursued a career as a jazz pianist, leading my jazz combo, the Eric Mintel Quartet. Over the years, I've had the honor of performing at prestigious venues such as the White House (invited by Presidents Clinton in 1998 and Obama in 2011), the Kennedy Center, National Gallery of Art, United Nations, various colleges, universities, libraries, high schools, churches, and jazz clubs.

With the paranormal always lingering in the background, I embarked on a new journey in 2016 by founding Bucks County Paranormal Investigations, which has since evolved into Eric Mintel Investigates due to increasing demand and our travels across the country, chronicled in this book. Together with my longtime friend and spirit medium Dominic Sattele, whom I've known since high school and who has been my companion on this journey since 2017, we've encountered and compiled cases of extraordinary phenomena. I firmly believe Dominic possesses a magnetism for these otherworldly situations, as you'll discover in the following pages.

Introduction:

**Case File: Lady in the Woods! 1997 Pineville,
PA Bucks County.**

I know I'm covering cases from 2016 onward
but I wanted to open with this story that
happened to me and still gives me chills to
this day.

As a jazz pianist and professional musician,
I'm often driving to various jobs all over Bucks
County and beyond. On this night in
November 1997, I was on my way to a steady
trio job I had at the time at a local restaurant
in Wycombe, PA. It was dark, cold and slightly
icy. As I'm driving, and I'm going at a pretty
good clip since I was running late, a deer
jumps out of nowhere and after no time to
react, I hit it! I slammed on the brakes and the
deer and I were sliding together as we came

to a stop on the road. I must have slid about 60 feet. I got out of the car and looked down at this poor deer. I felt terrible having just hit and killed this deer. It came out of nowhere.

Then, like a whisper out of the woods behind me, a female voice said "How's your hands?" I slowly turned around and saw this figure in white move over in front of the car. The lights of the car were on me to where I could only see her silhouette. Then to my shock, she bent down and took this 200 pound deer by the ear and dragged it off the road like it was light as a feather. She then said, "You better get off the road!" I got back in my car turned around and she was gone. I got to the gig still reeling from what happened and told the guys about it. They were happy I was okay. I went back the next day to see the area and thought maybe there was a house and someone was in the woods that spooked the deer. As I arrived in the location from the previous night there were no houses around, nothing but woods. To this day I still don't know what happened but I consider her my guardian angel.

Case File: UFO sighting January 2016 Stockton NJ.

It was a Wednesday night when we saw them! My fiancée, Sherry, and I were driving home after a night out along Route 32 (River Road) outside of New Hope, heading towards Centre Bridge. At the time, Sherry rented a farmhouse in Stockton, NJ, and we had to cross the bridge at Centre Bridge to reach Stockton. As we entered the bridge, which spans the famous Delaware River, I spotted five orange orbs that appeared out of thin air, about 300 feet above the bridge. They reminded me of swirling lava. This is a very populated area. Military flares were out of the question, as were drones. As I was seeing this, Sherry was getting a better look from the passenger side. In my mind, during these few seconds, I was thinking, could these be Chinese lanterns? After all, there is the

Centre Bridge Inn restaurant right there at the foot of the bridge as we entered. Maybe there was a wedding that night and they released them, but no. This was a Wednesday in January. It was cold too! As they appeared, they seemed to follow a search pattern, and then one by one started to disappear. I frantically got my camera out of my pocket and snapped two pics. The flash went off in the car, but on the second try, I was able to

capture the red orb before it disappeared. We both looked at each other and couldn't believe what we had just seen. I looked online the next day and was shocked to find other sightings similar to mine on that night or the day before in Harrisburg PA or later that night in Western PA.

A week later, Sherry was at the farmhouse, and I was on a gig. The farmhouse was set back from the road quite a ways. It was at least 500 feet from the house to the front of the road. In the field in front of the house, there was wheat. She said that on this particular night, she saw what looked like a ball of light bouncing along the tops of the wheat. She said it reminded her of the old days when people used to follow the bouncing ball on TV while singing songs on the Mitch Miller show. The light bounced along the wheat back and forth, then disappeared and was gone. She

tried to take a picture but couldn't.This
wouldn't be the last time UFO's were spotted
in the area.

Case File: Mystery at McCoole's Quakertown, Pa November 2018

Going from doing very fun, tongue-in-cheek videos to serious investigations started here at McCoole's Red Lion Inn. This beautiful restaurant, located in Quakertown, Pennsylvania, has an incredible haunted history. It was part of the Underground

Railroad, and the Fries Rebellion of 1799 took place there. The Fries Rebellion was an armed resistance by Pennsylvania-German farmers against the 1798 federal house tax, which was suppressed by soldiers. The leader, John Fries, was arrested for treason, sentenced to death, but was pardoned by President John Adams. There have also been other paranormal investigators who have seen "Peek a Boo" down in the basement. A small girl believed to be a slave whose spirit still runs through the restaurant. The night we arrived, staff was already buzzing about some new paranormal activity that happened just a few days before. One of the bartenders told us on camera that as she was pouring drinks, a bottle of vodka just jumped out of the speed rack. A speed rack is an enclosed half shelf close to the bartender that holds popular alcohol to make drinks fast. She also said she had her hoodie tugged at one night and turned around, but no one was there. Another server told us on camera about seeing flames go up and down a customer's sweater, only for them to disappear as quickly as they appeared. He also mentioned a Christmas ornament he personally witnessed, along with other servers, flying off the fireplace mantel. As we talked to him, something caught my eye, but I didn't pay any attention to it at the time until we saw the footage back at the office. More on that in a minute. The owner of the restaurant, Jan Hench, is not only one of the coolest people you will meet but also very community-oriented and does so much for the town of Quakertown. Jan gave us full access to explore all the paranormal hot spots and see what we could capture. Joining me that night was longtime friend and spirit medium Dominic Sattele, and longtime friend

and bassist in my quartet, Dave Antonow. We
unloaded the camera and equipment and
were ready to shoot. As I mentioned earlier,
when we were talking to the server who was
telling me about all of his experiences there,
what I didn't realize was that after looking at
that interview in post-production, I captured
an orb between the server and the camera. It
floated straight through. It was the beginning
of a night that would prove to be very
paranormal indeed. We started the
investigation in the basement. Dominic
wanted to check on the claims of this 'Peek a
Boo' spirit, and I had Dave stationed up in the
bar area to check the speed rack. After a while
of nothing happening in the bar area, Dave
made his way down to the basement and
checked out the area known as the jail cell
where captured slaves were once held. As
soon as Dave entered the area, he heard what

sounded like a woman crying. Dave alerted Dominic, and the two converged on the spot where Dave had heard the cry. I was examining the Underground Railroad tunnel that once led outside but was now caved in and impassable. Dominic and Dave didn't hear the cry again, and all three of us decided to go upstairs to investigate the dining room area, as well as the area where I had seen the orb during the interview.

As soon as we went upstairs, a palpable energy surged through the area. Dave continued to investigate and watch the bar area, Dominic was near the bathrooms and lobby and I was in the dining room. I slowly turned a corner and got surprised when I thought I saw two figures standing in the doorway but quickly realized it was a painting of two generals from the civil war.

After some fruitless attempts to capture evidence, we went over to McCoole's Arts and Events Center right next door to investigate claims of the spirit of a young boy. The story Jan told was That one day, an electrician was on his ladder hooking up a lighting system and saw a small boy running in circles around his ladder. Concerned, he called Jan and said, "There's a small boy up here running around; can you get his parents?" Jan had no idea what he was talking about because the area was completely closed off to the public. Jan said,'There's no boy up there!' When the electrician looked back down, the boy was gone. Later, it was found that there had been sightings of a small child who liked to sit on the stairs leading up to the dressing rooms. That's exactly where the electrician saw him. We decided to go check out that area and put a static camera on the area, unfortunately we never captured anything (the follow up investigation 5 years later would prove otherwise. More on that later). We did, however, talk to some workers at the theater who gave accounts of doors opening and knobs jiggling when no one was there. We wrapped up the investigation, and besides the orb activity, we didn't experience anything out of the ordinary (this time). This investigation proved to be just the tip of the paranormal iceberg with activity at such an incredible venue. We would return to McCoole's Red Lion Inn again.

Case File: Spirits at the General Warren. Malvern, Pa May 2019

I love forward-thinking people! Patrick Byrne, owner of the General Warren, is one of those people. I approached Patrick in January of 2019 about doing a feature for the General Warren for my show, which he agreed. A date was set for May of that year to start shooting.

On this day the team of Eric Mintel, Dominic Sattele, and Dave Antonow arrived at the General Warren and met with Patrick. We received an incredible history lesson about the General Warren from Patrick, who is not only incredibly knowledgeable about its history but also a most gracious and fun host to us for the day and eventual night investigation.

The General Warren dates back to 1745 and was established by George Ashton. During the American Revolution, the General Warren played a central role in what was known as the Philadelphia Campaign, where both British and Continental Troops used it as a landmark. In September 1777, the New Jersey Continental troops camped near the General Warren the night before the infamous Battle of the Clouds. Later that month, prior to the ill-fated Battle of Paoli, some civilians were briefly held in the General Warren in confinement as British General Charles Grey sought out

Continental General Anthony Wayne's troops.

There's a lot more history that you can learn about from our YouTube video of this case, "Spirits of the General Warren." Knowing this incredible history, I was so happy

to not only tell the story of the General Warren but also to hopefully experience any paranormal activity that Patrick would tell us about as we walked through the beautiful restaurant.

We set up our cameras and as Patrick walked through the locations with us, Dominic was manning the magnetometer, and as Patrick was speaking, we all collectively heard a crash coming from the dining room. Keep in mind, no one was working that day. Patrick had opened the restaurant just for us! After going

back into the dining room and seeing nothing
out of place, we continued the tour, which
included an on-site baking area and a beautiful
outdoor seating area that would be the site of
a very strange anomaly during the
investigation. Patrick then took us to the
'Franklin Room,' named after Ben Franklin,
who actually never visited the General

Warren. Patrick told us about lots of Activity surrounding this room included a handprint found on the window by the cleaning staff, who had no clue how it could've gotten there. Surprisingly, the magnetometer levels were low in this area, but as we pushed on, Patrick concluded the tour in the on-site baking area where they make all their own desserts and sweet treats. I asked Patrick if he could join us on the night investigation, to which he enthusiastically agreed.

We started in the dining room where we heard the loud bang earlier. As Dave and Dominic walked about, there was an eerie feeling that came over us. Patrick and I went outside to the seating area that we visited before. This area dated back to the original stone structure of the building. As Patrick and I were looking around we both heard what sounded like a drum. Could this have been residual energies from the troops who used to march past here beating their drums to keep in time? It was something we couldn't explain. We looked around the area but saw nothing and didn't hear it again.

Meanwhile Dave and Dominic were back inside and up in the Franklin room. We kept in radio contact the whole time. As Dave was on the second story investigating the other guest rooms available for over nighters, Dominic was no where to be found and couldn't be reached on the radio. I radioed Dave and told him to meet Patrick and I downstairs in the lobby. We once again tried to reach Dom but couldn't. Patrick had a pretty good idea where we may find him. We all collectively went back down in the basement area and as we were walking we heard what sounded like a gurgling sound. We looked at each other and as we got closer we realized it was coming from the on site baking area where as we opened the door, found Dominic eating a scone with tea! Thanks Dom!

After a good laugh Patrick took us to the oldest part of the General Warren, the sub basement where the foundations dated back to 1740. As Patrick was telling us more about the history of this space, again we heard a loud crash coming from upstairs right above us. Startled, both Patrick and I looked at each other! I asked him what room is above us and he said it was the main dining room. All four of us bolted upstairs to the dining room to see what happened but again we found nothing out of place. Patrick then remembered that a server was flambéing table side and the skillet flew out of her hand and crashed across the room on the ground. I asked "where that happened?" and he said "right here in the main dining room!"

Dominic checked the magnetometer but again found no fluctuations in the energy levels. Whatever made the crash was gone. We thanked Patrick for his hospitality and headed back to the office to look at the footage. To this day we are still wrapping our heads around that case which warrants another investigation.

Case File: Historical Haunt: The Inn at Jim Thorpe. Jim Thorpe, PA September 2019.

As a paranormal investigator, I was thrilled to have the opportunity to investigate the Inn at Jim Thorpe in Pennsylvania. The inn had gained a reputation for its haunted history, particularly in rooms 215 and 310. Joining me on this investigation was my trusted team member, Dave Antonow, and we were fortunate to have the assistance of the hotel manager, Nancy, and the owner, David.

Upon arriving at the inn, Nancy and David shared with us the spine-chilling stories that had been reported by guests.

Furniture rearranging itself, an icy cold grip felt by unsuspecting visitors, and sightings of a nurse in room 215 were just a few of the paranormal occurrences that had been witnessed. Additionally, room 310 was rumored to have served as a makeshift hospital during a past epidemic, adding to its haunted reputation.

Excitement filled the air as we set up our equipment in both rooms. EMF detectors, infrared cameras, and voice recorders were strategically placed to capture any signs of paranormal activity. We were all eager to uncover the truth behind the eerie happenings.

Dave and I decided to begin our investigation in room 215, while the rest of the team focused on room 310. As we entered the room, a sense of unease washed over us. The atmosphere felt heavy, and we could almost sense a presence lingering in the air. We prepared ourselves for a night of exploration.

Almost immediately, we experienced a drastic drop in temperature. Despite the absence of any drafts, an icy cold grip seemed to envelop the room, causing us to shiver.

Meanwhile, in room 310, the rest of the team reported feeling a distinct presence. Whispers and faint cries echoed through the room, reminiscent of its past as a makeshift hospital. The EMF detectors registered unusual spikes, indicating the presence of spiritual energy.

Throughout the investigation, we conducted an EVP session, hoping to communicate with any spirits present. We asked questions and patiently awaited responses. We did capture a female voice that seemed to be humming a song. More evidence revealing fragments of the inn's haunted history.

As the night progressed, we regrouped to share our findings. As we were ready to go over the findings a gentleman came up to me and asked if I had seen the video of the cup that moved behind the bar. He pulled out his phone and showed me the video. I was shocked to see this metal cup move by an unknown force. The bartender was also startled on the video. I asked him to send me the video. The evidence we had collected was substantial, including EVPs, temperature fluctuations, and visual anomalies captured on camera. We were thrilled with the results, as they provided undeniable proof of the paranormal activity reported in rooms 215 and 310.

After concluding our investigation, I met with Nancy and David to present our findings. They were both fascinated and slightly unnerved by the evidence we had gathered. They expressed their gratitude for shedding light on the inn's haunted reputation and assured

us that they would continue sharing these stories with future guests.

Our investigation at the Inn at Jim Thorpe had not only confirmed the reports of paranormal activity in rooms 215 and 310 but also deepened our understanding of the inn's haunted history. The collaboration between my team, Nancy, and David had brought forth compelling evidence, leaving no doubt that the inn was indeed a hotspot for supernatural encounters.

Case File: The Haunting of Hill View Manor
New Castle, PA November 2020

A drive from Bucks County Pennsylvania to New Castle through beautiful blue skies one min to a white out blizzard the next, we arrived after the 5 hour drive to this historical paranormal hot spot. The air hung heavy with anticipation as we approached the foreboding entrance of Hill View Manor. The immense structure, stretching across a staggering 85,000 square feet, cast a dark shadow over the grounds. Rumors of its haunted nature had ignited a collective curiosity, compelling us to venture inside and unravel the enigma that enveloped its walls.

After meeting with Carrie, the owner of Hill View Manor, we were given full access to explore and were taken on a tour where we learned a lot about the history of this storied place. As we crossed the threshold, the sheer magnitude of Hill View Manor struck us with awe. Its grandeur was overshadowed only by the mysteries concealed within its expansive rooms and echoing hallways. There was an undeniable story to be told, and we were determined to unearth its secrets.

From the very beginning, a haunting presence gripped us. Cold spots materialized seemingly out of thin air, sending shivers down our spines. It felt as if the spirits of the past were still trapped within, refusing to relinquish their hold on this earthly plane.

Armed with cutting-edge equipment, we embarked on our investigation, accompanied by our trusted team members. Dominic Sattele, a renowned spirit medium, lent his expertise, heightening the sense of intrigue and anticipation. His abilities to communicate with the other side added an extra layer of mystique to our endeavor.

As we traversed the dimly lit hallways, the weight of the past pressed upon us. Shadows danced in our peripheral vision, and eerie echoes reverberated through the empty corridors. It was during one such exploration that Dominic's perceptive senses led us to a particularly active area. In the distance, we glimpsed a shadowy figure, ethereal and transient. Its presence sent a chill down our spines, reminding us that we were not alone.

Undeterred by the unsettling encounters, we pressed on, following the trail of spectral energy that permeated the manor. Dominic's connection to the spirit world grew stronger, and he described vivid encounters with the apparition of an orderly who once worked there.

The weight of history was palpable as we delved deeper into the mysteries of Hill View Manor. Each step brought us closer to understanding the tangled web of spirits that resided here.

Hill View Manor stands as a testament to the rich history of New Castle, Pennsylvania, but within its walls, that history took on a spectral form. The lingering presence of the spirits became an undeniable reality, reminding us that there is more to this world than meets the eye. The manor became a portal—a gateway to the unknown—where the boundaries between the living and the dead blurred.

As our investigation neared its conclusion, a mixture of awe, fascination, and reverence enveloped us. The evidence we had gathered—the shadow figures, the cold spots, the heat signatures—was undeniable proof of the paranormal activity that permeated Hill View Manor. We knew that this place would forever captivate the curious, beckoning them to embark on their own journey of discovery. Perhaps they, too, would catch a glimpse of the otherworldly residents who still wandered within its hallowed halls.

With our findings in hand, we bid farewell to the haunted manor, aware that its secrets would endure long after we had departed. Hill View Manor would forever be etched in our memories, a testament to the ethereal and an invitation to those who dared to explore its haunted depths.

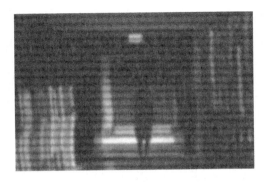

Case File: New Jerseys Roswell August 2019
Monmouth, New Jersey

One of my favorite shows from 2008-2009 was
UFO Hunters with Bill Birnes. I remember
saying to myself, one day I'm going to have my
own paranormal tv show and I want to work
with Bill. Turns out Bill lives a few miles away

from me as I ran into him at a local coffee
shop in 2013. In 2019 reached out to Bill and
asked if he wanted to do a video on some UFO

sightings in NJ. To my delight he agreed! Dream accomplished!

We met, and I drove us to meet UFO witness and retired IT guy Joe Foster in Monmouth, NJ, who would tell us a most fascinating story of three sightings that happened in 1958, 1970, and 2002. On this particular day in August 2019, it must have been over 100 degrees. We arrived at Dorbrook Park and met Joe. We stood at the epicenter of the Monmouth UFO sightings, our minds brimming with curiosity and determination. Together, we embarked on a quest to uncover the truth behind the unexplained events that had unfolded in this enigmatic corner of New Jersey.

Joe Foster, with his firsthand encounters and unwavering resolve, led the way. He recounted his experiences with vivid detail, starting with the silver sphere he witnessed soaring across the Monmouth skies in 1958. The image of that otherworldly object burned into his memory, igniting a lifelong pursuit of the truth.

Bill Birnes, an expert in the field of UFO research, listened intently, his analytical mind absorbing every word. He knew that Joe's sightings were not isolated incidents but part of a larger tapestry of strangeness that spanned decades.

"As fascinating as your sighting in 1958 is, Joe," Eric Mintel began, "we have to delve deeper. There's a common thread connecting these sightings. In 1958, you mentioned the jammed phone lines during your UFO event. Tell us more about that."

Joe recollected the events of 1958. "It was a remarkable day," he said. "Multiple witnesses reported seeing a bright, glowing object in the sky. But what was even more perplexing was the disruption it caused to the town's communication systems. Phone lines were jammed, and people were unable to reach emergency services. It was as if the presence of the UFO was interfering with our technology."

Bill Birnes nodded, his mind already racing with possibilities. "This isn't the first time we've come across reports of UFOs interfering with electronic devices," he said. "There's a long history of these incidents, suggesting a connection between these objects and their effects on our technology."

As they stood there, contemplating the implications of these sightings, their attention shifted to the events of 1970. Joe had mentioned a landed UFO in a secluded swamp. It was a remarkable incident that left an indelible mark on Monmouth's UFO chronicles.

"Joe, can you tell us more about the landed UFO in 1970?" Eric inquired, his curiosity piqued.

Joe took a deep breath, reliving that fateful day. "I stumbled upon the story of the UFO landing in a secluded swamp nearby," he explained. "The energy emanating from it was palpable, almost magnetic. The police officer on patrol that day couldn't believe his eyes. It was a tangible confirmation that these sightings were more than just lights in the sky. As he approached the area where the UFO landed, he saw a brilliant flash and upon getting out of his car, he stated that he saw landing marks in the field near the swamp where the alleged craft landed. There was something real, something tangible happening right here in Monmouth."

Bill Birnes exchanged a knowing glance with Eric. "The presence of magnetism is a significant detail," he said. "We've come across similar reports in other UFO cases. It suggests that these

objects generate electromagnetic fields, which could explain their effects on technology and perhaps even the human body."

Their investigation was taking shape, the pieces of the puzzle coming together. But there was one more enigma they couldn't ignore—the crop circle that had materialized in Dorbrook Park in 2002. It was a phenomenon that had left the community in awe, with intricate patterns etched into the soil overnight.

"Joe, the crop circle at Dorbrook Park in 2002 is a fascinating element of this story," Eric noted. "Do you have any insights into its appearance?"

Joe's eyes lit up. "I did some research and discovered that the that the crop circle was not a hoax but rather a result of an external force interacting with the environment." The movie "Signs" had recently been released and the skeptics thought it was some kind of hoax but no explanation has ever been provided to this day. Eric took some soils samples, hopeful that it would be tested for any magnetite.

Bill Birnes nodded, his excitement building. "Magnetite is often associated with UFO-related phenomena," he explained. "Its presence could indicate a direct connection between the UFO sightings, the landed craft, and the crop circle. We might be on the brink of unraveling something truly extraordinary here."

As the trio stood there, surrounded by the echoes of Monmouth's UFO chronicles, a newfound sense of purpose and urgency gripped them. The silver sphere, the jammed phone lines, the landed UFO, the magnetite-infused soil—all the pieces were coming together, revealing a larger story of unknown origins and untold possibilities.

With Joe Foster's experiences as their guide, Eric Mintel and Bill Birnes vowed to push forward, unearthing the truth that lay hidden within Monmouth's UFO sightings. The mysteries were still there, but armed with determination, expertise, and the flame of curiosity, we were prepared to journey deeper into the heart of the unknown. As Bill and I got back in the car he was fascinated by the case and said "I think this is New Jersey's Roswell!

Case File: Mysteries at the Mauch Chunk Opera House. Jim Thorpe, PA November 2019

The Mauch Chunk Opera House in Jim Thorpe, Pennsylvania, is caught up in a perplexing web of supernatural events. Together with renowned paranormal

investigator Bill Birnes, we delved into the mysteries that surrounded this historic venue.

Vince, a talented musician and singer, owns the Opera House, and he entrusted me and Bill with a thorough investigation. Little did I know that our journey would take an unexpected turn into the realm of the paranormal. We were determined to uncover the truth behind the reports of strange phenomena and spectral sightings that had been haunting this venue for years.

As Vince told us about a shadow figure he saw on the balcony we immediately ventured into the balcony area, the atmosphere grew thick with anticipation. The story Vince told played like a reel in my mind, and I braced myself for what lay ahead. Bill, armed with the magnetometer, scanned the room, his trained eyes searching for any signs of paranormal activity.

Suddenly, I felt a chill crawl up my spine, as if an unseen presence had descended upon us. It was during post production that our camera captured something remarkable—two ethereal orbs of light shot upwards from Vince's head. I couldn't believe my eyes. I found myself questioning the nature of these strange phenomena.

We then met with manager Dan who told us his story of a feeling of someone looking over his shoulder one night while he was sweeping the stage. He felt it was coming from the balcony. Bill and I exchanged astonished glances, knowing that we had stumbled upon something truly extraordinary. We continued our investigation, delving deeper into the history of the Opera House and its connection to these spirits.

Over the course of our exploration, we
discovered accounts of a ghostly figure,
believed to be a former projectionist and his
wife, who roamed the halls. Visitors and staff
members shared stories of feeling an
inexplicable presence, as if someone was
watching them, and witnessing fleeting
apparitions out of the corner of their eyes.

The enigmatic orbs that emanated from
Vince's head became a focal point of our
research. We sought answers, scouring
historical records, consulting experts, and

documenting every peculiar occurrence. The Opera House had become a hub of artistic expression and a portal into the supernatural.

As our investigation progressed, we uncovered a pattern—a strange energy that seemed to envelop the balcony area. It was as if the spirits of the past were drawn to this space, leaving behind traces of their existence.

The Mauch Chunk Opera House had transformed into a place where artistic performances and spectral encounters intertwined, blurring the lines between the tangible and the ethereal. What mysteries resided within these walls?

Today, the Mauch Chunk Opera House stands as a testament to Jim Thorpe and it's enduring legacy of super athlete Jim Thorpe, the creative spirit of Vince, and the enigmatic forces that continue to captivate those who cross its threshold. The journey I embarked on with Bill Birnes again opened my eyes to the profound connection between art, history, and the unexplained. In this timeless venue, the mysteries of the past are eternally intertwined with the present, reminding us that the truth often lies beyond what our rational minds can comprehend. We will return.

Case File: The Beast of Bray Road: Alive and Well. Elkhorn, WI October 2021

As I boarded the plane in Philadelphia with high school buddy and spirit medium Dominic Sattele, I felt a mix of excitement and anticipation for our journey to Elkhorn. Our destination was to meet up with the Wisconsin paranormal team members, Ellen Collins and Scott Chrysler. Upon arrival, we were introduced to Lee Hample, who had

some fascinating insights to share. We arrived at Lee's farm in the early afternoon that day.

Lee talked to our team about seeing the red glowing eyes, the hair samples that appeared translucent under a microscope, a discovery that immediately piqued our curiosity. With this intriguing information, our investigation into the enigmatic Beast of Bray Road began in earnest.

The night of the investigation the chilling wind cut through the night air as my team and

I stood at the edge of Lee's hayfield. This case had intrigued me like no other in my career with Eric Mintel Investigates. Dominic Sattele, who had an uncanny knack for sensing the supernatural, was as eager as I was to explore the mysteries that Lee Hampel's evidence had led us to. This was way out of his wheelhouse but he was game!

Beside us was our producer, Ellen Collins, who possessed a wealth of knowledge about the mysterious tapetum lucidum phenomenon regarding eye shine, and her son, Scott, who was a drone operator and would help us capture any unexplained activity from above. We were a tight-knit team, ready to tackle the unknown.

As the sun dipped below the horizon, the hayfield took on an eerie aura. The stories we had heard from Lee Hampel pointed to the existence of the elusive Beast of Bray Road, a creature rumored to be 6 to 7 feet tall and walk on two legs. This cryptid was known to roam these very fields. Bray Road is only two tenths of a mile from Lee's hayfield. Armed with our equipment and a sense of excitement, we stepped into the unknown. It was around 8:30pm October 3, 2021.

We arrived on four-wheelers and reached the bait area, a corner in Lee's field where he has

had the most activity. I had placed steak bones earlier in the day, and all afternoon I wondered if that was such a good idea. Suddenly, Dominic happened to look up and say "What the hell is that!?" We all looked up and saw a bright white glowing object in the

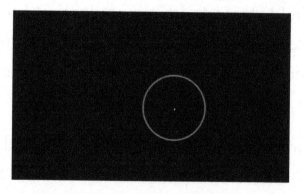

sky slowly going over the field above us. It was a UFO, no doubt. As we are trying to wrap our heads around what it could be, it made a 45 degree angle and blinked out, leaving us baffled.

Right after the UFO, we heard a howl in the distance. Dominic and I looked at each other. Ellen was still looking at the sky. Then, we heard another howl, closer this time. Dominic said to Ellen, who was still looking at the sky, 'Are you hearing these howls?' She said, 'Yes, they're coming from over there!' As soon as Ellen said that, we all heard a third howl, which was more like a scream-growl-yell combination that sounded like a man screaming. It was only about 100 yards from us. We were shocked. What were we hearing? It was louder on-site, but our small

microphones managed to capture this bone-chilling howl. Next, a weird mist came up from the field and started to mess with our electronics. Still wrapping our heads around what we just heard, Dominic told the team to be quiet as he heard rustling sounds behind us. There was no wind at all on this night. We asked Scott to shine the light towards where we heard the howls, and suddenly we saw two yellow eyes about 6 to 7 feet up in the corn line, shifting positions and looking at us. It was time to go! We got on the four-wheelers that brought us down to the 35-acre field and made the trek back to Lee's barn.

Back at the hotel, Ellen's expertise came into play as she pointed out tapetum lucidum reflections from creatures' eyes. The evidence was mounting, confirming that something unnatural was indeed present. We recapped what happened as we sat at the hotel in Elkhorn. That night, the entire town of Elkhorn lost power. That morning, Lee sent me a message saying that the trail cameras he had positioned in the field the previous night were not working. He said it was like something turned them off at 5 PM and didn't come back on again until 7 AM that morning. Nothing was captured on the trail cam. Not us and certainly not the creature. The Beast of Bray Road remained elusive. The UFO, the howls, the mist and the eye shine across the hayfield left us with more questions than answers. We had only scratched the surface of the this cryptid and I couldn't wait to return, to delve deeper into the heart of the unexplained.

This case would become one of the most memorable chapters in this book. The Beast of Bray Road is alive and well in Elkhorn. This will forever remain etched in my mind, a testament to what we experienced and the mysterious forces that lie just beyond the veil of our reality.

Case file: On the Watch for Squatch Part 1.
October 11, 2021

A week after we came back from Elkhorn, we decided to head to the New Jersey Pine Barrens to investigate recent Bigfoot sightings in the Wharton State Forest area. Again, Dominic Sattele joined me on this investigation, which was also outside his wheelhouse as a spirit medium.

"Hunting cryptids? I usually get 'What have you dragged me into now, Mintel!?' which we always chuckle at. On this night, we met up with Bigfoot researchers Eric Spinner and Art Mack in Medford, New Jersey. Eric took us to an area called the 'Bowl' where he has been getting a lot of activity—footprints, hair samples, wood knocks, and more. It was a clear night, with the moon at about a quarter, giving the area an eerie atmosphere. Thanks to Dominic's truck, we drove about five miles into the forest on fire roads to reach the area called the Bowl. It was around 7:30 PM when we arrived at the location. As soon as we got out of the truck, an intense feeling of isolation and silence hit me. We were literally in the middle of

nowhere. We set up chairs at our makeshift base camp, which was smack dab in the middle of the bowl. We talked about how

Eric and Art conduct their research and what tools they use, in addition to audio and thermal imaging. Dominic and Art were having a philosophical discussion on the Bigfoot and UFO connection when suddenly we all heard a whoop coming from the forest behind us! I couldn't believe it! Whenever I watch those Bigfoot shows, I always hear people whooping and hollering for Bigfoot, and I say to myself, 'Is that what they really sound like? I'll be damned if that's not what we heard!' Eric had high-powered audio going at that exact time, which also caught the whoop. Next, Eric's wife, Heather, answered back with her own whoop, which to our amazement was answered back not once, but five times! Playing the footage back, you can definitely hear the whoops on the video. We were all now on high alert! We

THE TEAM KEEPS HEARING WHOOPING SOUNDS AND RUSTLING SOUNDS.

tried more whoops, but whatever was there was now gone. Eric showed us how he does tree knocks. Tree knocks are thought to be a way that Bigfoot communicates. As he was ready to hit the tree with his squatch stick, we all heard another whoop! After a few hours, we didn't get any more activity and decided to wrap up the investigation. The activity was off the charts that night and changed my whole perspective on the Bigfoot and cryptid phenomena. We would return again in September 2023!

Case file: Hallowed Grounds at the Homestead Boyertown, PA August, 2022

On a warm day in August, Dominic Sattele and I pulled into Boyertown Pennsylvania and into New Spirit Old Soul. New Spirit Old Soul is a fun architectural salvage company known for their pieces and incredible history. We met with Beth and Jacob, the owners and together we sat down and they told me about how they found this business they had been driving by for years and as Beth put it, I dreamt this would be my business so I made an offer an offer and they accepted. Attached to this wonderful homestead is a fully functioning farmhouse dating back to 1749. The farmhouse always held some strange unearthly energy that Beth connected to but she couldn't quite figure out what it was but knew it was coming from the bedroom upstairs.

A friend of Beth's named Rene also had strong ties to the energy emanating from the farmhouse. So much energy that one day while Rene was on the property she saw an apparition of a woman gesturing her to come to the summer kitchen, another beautiful building on the property. After my interview with Beth and Jacob I went to look for Dominic who was touring the grounds outside. He too said he saw the spirit of a woman and the spirit of a little boy at the summer kitchen and saw the little boy playing in the springhouse. Keep in mind Dominic was no where around when Rene told me her experience. That night we gathered in the kitchen of the farmhouse to begin the nights

investigation. The energy was at an all time
high and anxiety palpable. Dominic was also
sensing, through spirit, a woman upstairs in
one of the bedrooms that was calling out to
him.

With the lights off and with only night vision in
the camera to see by, we cautiously started to
make our way up the stairs with Beth, Jacob,
Todd, Rene and about 4 other guests in tow
who wanted to be involved in the

investigation. In hindsight, having that many people there was probably not a good idea because of what that spirit did next! We arrived at the top of the stairs and Dominic asked what bedroom this was and was this the room Beth was feeling the energy from? Beth said yes this was the room and said it was the main bedroom. I took the magnetometer to check for any residual energies and like clockwork the meter was going up and down hitting a .4 to .9. Keep in mind there is no wifi or any electrical wirings as such in this farmhouse, it's practically as it was back in the 1700's. As we scanned over the bedroom I passed by a low dresser and suddenly saw the plants move to my right. I said to everyone "I don't want to alarm anyone but I just saw that vase with the plants move!" to which Beth answered strongly "I did not put that there, that was not there, I know where things are in this room and I did not put that there!!!" as she was explaining wildly she suddenly started to seize up and began to hyperventilate! She was, as we say bumrushed by the spirit in that

bedroom. We got Beth out of there and into the adjoining hallway to help her calm down. Jacob was trying to comfort her, and we were asking her what happened in that moment. She said that she had a wash of emotions all over her and she got completely overwhelmed by it. We made our way out of the bedroom and back downstairs.

Getting our bearings again, we recapped what just happened, and by this time Beth was now calm. Suddenly, a story began to unfold of who the spirit was!Dominic was told through spirit that this entity was a woman named Elizabeth. She was married to the owner of the home, with whom he had an affair with a worker on the property, and they had a child together. Elizabeth had a son and a daughter, but her son died at a very early age and is believed to be buried somewhere on the property. Dominic said that the spirit of Elizabeth was saying, 'Why did my son die and his brat live?' This case was one of the most heart-wrenching ones we did. Seeing Beth overwhelmed with that burst of emotional energy and then trying to come down from it was not only frightening but eye-opening to the world of what spirits want to tell us.

Case file: On the Watch for Squatch Part 2
September 2, 2023

On September 2, 2023, Dominic Sattele and I once again set off to follow up on our 2021 investigation of Bigfoot in the New Jersey Pine Barrens, as you just read in the previous chapter. The day was a Saturday, September 2, 2023. The weather was clear, and an air of trepidation hit us as we ventured further into the Pine Barrens, particularly the Wharton State Forest. We arrived around 4:30 PM and met our friend and Bigfoot researcher, Art Mack. Eric Spinner was on his way. This time, we wanted to utilize Dominic's gifts more. Eric Spinner had the idea: what if Bigfoot is a ghost! The idea was very intriguing but maybe we were looking in the wrong direction the whole time. Nevertheless Eric arrived and we went back to the Bowl, where we had been two years earlier, and set up base camp.

Nighttime seemed to come up on us quickly. Before we knew it there was an eerie chill in the air and the forest around us faded into blackness. I must admit on

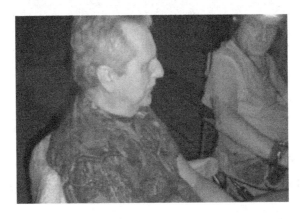

this night's investigation I was a little more on edge than the last time we visited. As we sat at basecamp talking about the investigation and what we would do first the lights that Eric had brought were drained mysteriously of their battery. Dominic's apple watch was also drained and my phone was also drained and showing low power after if was fully charged.

That was the first inclination I should have had that something was around us on this fateful night.

It grew darker and we decided to go back down a trail near basecamp to listen and check out the area. The only thing we heard was a bird, a whippoorwill. We walked back to base camp, sat down and let Dominic tune in on the area. Earlier Dominic realized that something was attached to Art. Art has also been battling cancer and to see his strength through the difficult times was truly inspirational. Dominic figured out that Art is connected to Sasquatch in way that the Sasquatch is seeing through Art's eyes. This would prove to have devastating consequences in a few moments. As Art is sitting in the circle he suddenly said "Guys I don't know if it's the medication I'm taking but my heart is really racing right now!" as soon as he said that I heard a branch crack behind us, Eric's daughter Anastasia was on camera, she too turned in the direction and there we all

saw a branch moving erratically like something was just standing there watching us.

I jumped up and suddenly saw two yellow eyes looking back at us about 6 to 7 feet up then disappeared. Truly (besides the Beast of Bray Road) one of the spookiest nights we ever had. We went to the area to see if we could see tracks but there was too much leaf litter. Whatever it was saw us, then bolted back to the swamp in this once beautiful cedar forest. The rest of the evening was

uneventful but we will never forget that crack of the branch and the two yellow eyes looking down on us! This investigation changed my whole perspective on Bigfoot and what is lurking out there in the dark! We are not done with this investigation. There is so much more to discover. By the way, Art was fine.

Case file: Chills at Cheney Hall Manchester, CT March 2022

As is usually the case, I drag Dominic all over creation. On this day our journey found us in Manchester, CT to investigate an incredible theater I have performed at over the years called Cheney Hall. Cheney Hall, little did I know how haunted it is! We arrived and met with director Dwayne Harris who took us on a tour of the theater and all the rooms. We were downstairs by the dressing room and Dominic was feeling some very very strange energy coming from that room. That room would make itself known later during the investigation. After the tour Dominic went outside to tune in on the grounds and Dwayne and I sat down as he told me some incredible stories of Cheney Hall and it's history. Cheney Hall was a makeshift hospital during the Spanish flu epidemic of 1920 and how many people died here. How odd it was that we were doing this investigation 100 years later during another crazy epidemic called Covid19. I then met with a worker at the theater who told me about sightings of a

woman's shadow on the catwalks, a phenomenon witnessed by multiple people over the years. She also shared stories about Fred, the heart of the theater and its chief set designer, who poured his heart and soul into numerous productions. Cheney Hall was constructed by the Cheney brothers, renowned silk manufacturers who made significant contributions to Manchester. In fact, Susan B. Anthony delivered a speech about the suffragette movement on Cheney Hall's front porch in the late 1800s. Dominic began sensing spiritual impressions immediately upon entering the theater, visualizing it filled with beds or bunk beds and noticing blood on the floor. Acknowledging his impressions, I affirmed he was correct, as this area had functioned as a makeshift hospital during the Spanish flu. As our investigation progressed, the energy intensified with the deepening night. Intrigued by reports of shadows on the catwalk, I ascended while Dominic returned to explore the earlier unsettling energy in the dressing room. We maintained communication via radio; I carried the magnetometer, while Dominic used the EVP recorder to capture any disembodied sounds.

On the catwalk, the magnetometer surged
with energy readings ranging from 3.0 to 11.
Meanwhile, in the now darkened dressing
room, Dominic moved cautiously. Our
cameraman followed closely as Dominic
turned on the EVP and queried, 'Is anyone
here? If you're here, show me a sign!' After a
brief pause, three distinct knocks echoed
through the room, startling Dominic as he
quickly reacted to the startling activity. You
could see he was very startled and got on the

radio and told me in so many words to get my
ass down there!! I ran down from the catwalk

to the dressing room and saw Dominic completely freaked out. I've only seen him like this a few times. What those knocks were we have no idea but later on we found out that another worker also had the same thing happen to him. We recapped the nights events with Dwayne who was blown away by our findings. We then headed back to Bucks County. We held a screening of Chills at Cheney Hall in January 2023 to a packed house of over 300 people, with another 100 participating in the ghost tour that accompanied it. Cheney Hall holds many more secrets yet to be revealed, and we look forward to returning.

Case file: The Beast of Bryn Athyn. Bryn Athyn, PA September 2022

Werewolf? Dogman? Are they one and the same? I had heard of such creatures before, but like the Beast of Bray Road, I hadn't delved into the subject until now. My good friend and ufologist Tom Carey took a keen interest in these sightings of a Dogman, called the Beast of Bryn Athyn, near his hometown in

Pennsylvania. Tom sunk his teeth into this cryptid like a dog biting into a meaty bone! He was hooked! Tom reached out to me after

witnessing what we encountered in Elkhorn, Wisconsin, and proposed an investigation on this elusive cryptid. I agreed and soon arrived at Tom's place, ready to go.

Tom had lined up several witnesses willing to go on camera to discuss their sightings of this creature, so we set out to meet them. On a particularly hot day, we met with a witness who claimed to have seen this creature emerging from a vortex in the field we were now in. He said that he also saw UFO lights in the shape of a person stationary over the same field. He has had several UFO encounters along with the Dogman in this

area and both Tom and I now believe he is connected to this phenomenon. We thanked him and he left. We headed to the area of the supposed vortex, but as we approached, Tom struggled and eventually went down on his knees. I told him to stay put while I fetched the car to drive closer. Thankfully, once he was in the air conditioning, he felt better. Could the energy of the area have affected Tom?

Next, we met with a woman who, in 1995, had seen this creature with a group of college friends. She described it as walking upright initially, appearing to glide, but then dropping down on all fours and disappearing quickly. This description matched sightings of the Beast of Bray Road. It turns out there are numerous Dogman sightings across the country, all describing a very similar creature.

Afterwards, we met Rich Show, who recounted an incident from 1990. He was sitting on a bench in the baseball field behind the local church when he saw an 8-foot shadow emerge from the trees, move to center field, return to the trees, and then reappear in center field again. He described it as gliding. Two witnesses who didn't know each other, yet they described the same thing.

Rich mentioned that he and his friend heard it moving into the brush across from the field and chased after it. They stopped in their tracks when they heard it coming back

Drawing by
Richard Show

7ft.

towards them as Rich heard this heavy something crashing through the underbrush. They never saw it again but the memory lives on. We all decided to do a night investigation near the area Rich had his sighting as well as the woman's sighting of the creature near Bryn Athyn Cathedral.

I also brought Dominic Sattele out on this one to see what the spiritual connections could be to this cryptid. Dominic went out into the field where the woman had her sighting and right in that area the magnetometer was going off the charts. We never had this happen before in an area in

the middle of a field. Tom Carey said that another witness called him earlier that day to tell him that they had seen this creature in the area we were now in. They said it was appearing and disappearing in several spots all over the field like the flash snap shots of a camera. Could this creature be using portals to come in and out of our reality?

After getting no other activity we went over to the baseball field where Rich had his sighting. As we approached, Rich began to get goosebumps. The encounter had profoundly affected him, and we were determined to uncover more. Despite using the magnetometer and a compass, neither device detected anything unusual in the area where Rich had seen the creature many years ago.

Whatever they had encountered seemed to have vanished, but our investigation shed light on these cryptids that appear across different parts of the world. We are now planning a follow-up investigation.

Case file: UFO's Over Bucks County
2021/2023

In January of 2023, we started investigating numerous reports from Bucks County, Pennsylvania, particularly in Doylestown. I received a message from a woman named Leslie who described an incident from April 2021. She woke up in the middle of the night and looked out her window to see stationary white lights hovering above nearby Lake Galena near her home. Leslie managed to capture video footage of the lights, which remains compelling to this day. The lights appeared stationary, moving only slightly but never wavering from their positions to much. I ruled out Star link satellites because they move in a straight line but these were stationary and at different heights. Dominic and I met with Leslie at the site a few days later. To be visiting Leslie at the site just days after such an amazing encounter was extraordinary. We sat and talked with her for a while on a beautiful day, and she was just as confused about what she saw as we were. Having seen videos like that before, everything Leslie told us we believed because other folks have been having similar encounters.

In August of 2022, I received a message from a woman on Facebook. She recounted closing her guest room windows when she noticed a low, brightly lit object hovering silently just outside. She even sent me a drawing, which

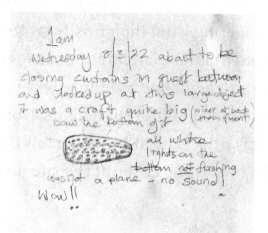

resembled the classic UFO shape. These reports continue to add to the intrigue surrounding the phenomena in Bucks County.

I had received a video from a nurse (Nicole) from Doylestown Hospital who said she was looking out a window during her break and noticed three lights in a triangular formation over Rt 611 during the midday. She was smart to pull out the cell phone and get video of what she was seeing. She asked a co-worker if she too saw the lights and the co-worker also confirmed the sighting and saw what Nicole was seeing. Another very compelling video.

Towards the end of 2022 reports of not only high level balloons being shot down over our air space flourished in the news but also some other objects that were seen flying in our airspace that were not balloons. Small objects the size of a car was reported hovering over the Yukon. These reports quickly went silent. In January 2023, our decision to delve deeper into this phenomenon stemmed from a message I received from Mitch Sherman in Ottsville, Pennsylvania. Mitch shared that for the past three years, he had been witnessing a similar sight: a low-flying, brightly lit object

hovering over his home. Intrigued by his account, Dominic and I felt compelled to meet Mitch and his wife Robin, who had an incredible story to share and one of possible contact. We arrived at the Sherman residence and were met with warmth from Mitch and Robin who have since become great friends. Mitch told us that for the last three years he and Robin have been seeing this brightly lit object low in the sky but have also seen smaller objects coming out of the larger light on several occasions. On one occasion Robin and Mitch were outside when they saw the light again. Mitch went inside to get his binoculars and as he did Robin said that a small light the size of a finger came right up to her face and then shot off in an instant. Robin yelled for Mitch to see but by the time he got out there it was gone but not before Mitch captured an incredible video which is clearly a ball of light moving slowly over their home.

Mitch said that these occurrences were happening during the months of May June or July. We came back in mid May of 2023 to do a night investigation. The night was clear and

the stars were out. We checked the star maps
and checked for satellites going over head
but nothing on this night. Mitch decided to
get a laser pointer and show us exactly where
he saw the lights come from the first time. As
soon as he showed us in the sky where he first
saw the lights, an object blinked on for a few
seconds lighting up next to the pointer. We
were able to capture it on video. It was truly

amazing to see this anomaly and get it on
video. The rest of the evening we didn't see
anything else but I told Mitch to call us

immediately if it shows up again! Since this case more and more UFO's and USO's (unidentified submerged objects) have made the news and fueled public interest. The mystery deepens and this is something we will continue to look into.

Case file: What Waits at the Water Wheel Tavern? Doylestown, PA March 2023.

The Water Wheel Tavern in Doylestown, PA, has a storied history as a grist mill, a stop for George Washington and his troops en route to Valley Forge, and later as a series of restaurants and inns. Nestled in a picturesque landscape, the Water Wheel has been a community staple for years, and it's also known for its array of ghost stories. Once again, spirit medium Dominic Sattele was on the case, but joining us for the first time was psychic medium Julie Kraus. I had heard of Julie from several people who had incredible results with her, and she came highly recommended. Julie enthusiastically agreed to join us.

As soon as the three of us entered the tavern Julie felt chills on top of her head which she

said was spirit trying to connect with her.
Manager Jim told me earlier about several
incidents that happened in the tavern. A
woman was inquiring about a private
party and Jim took her down stairs to the
cellar bar but as he reached the bottom of the
stairs he sensed she wasn't behind him. He
turned around and saw the woman at the top
of the stairs who said to Jim, "there's a spirit
down there with you and it does not like you!"
Jim has had other encounters where he was in
his office upstairs and heard barstools being

moved around only to look down and see no one there but the stools were rearranged. Dominic and Julie had no idea of any of this paranormal activity. I always try to get them on camera going to a hot spot that speaks to them that just happens to be an area where others have had encounters with the otherworldly. At this sight a few years ago there was also a dog man sighting on the grounds of the Water Wheel. An upright 7 foot canine walking and jumping on tow legs was seen by a couple driving past the restaurant that jumped into the nearby woods. The case remains open and unsolved.

It was intriguing how Julie was feeling animal energy when all three of us were in the cellar bar. On the stairs leading down to the bar both Julie and Dominic were feeling strong energy at the top of the stairs. When I placed the magnetometer in the area it went off the

charts. Julie had to leave but not before
telling us that she also felt the spirit of a

woman and child near the fireplace. Julie also
said she heard heavy weeping coming from
the woman. Jim told me earlier that people
have seen a woman sitting at a table by the
fireplace but then in an instant disappears.
Could this be the woman looking for her
child? Dominic and I went back down to the
cellar bar but before we did, Dominic sensed
the spirit of the woman at the table again so
we decided to do an evp. Unfortunately we
did not hear anything but our flashlights kept

going off and on which you can clearly see on our video. Once down in the cellar bar I decided to take some video with my phone. I pointed it up the stairs where we were getting the heavy energy readings and like clockwork we began getting orbs. This was not dust nor

bugs. It was March and it was cold. The magnetometer was also spoiling. Clearly something was down there with us. We wrapped up the investigation with no further evidence. We had a screening event of the video to a packed house of fans who were thrilled with the investigation. There is a lot

more to be done there but for the time being
we will let the spirits rest.

Case file: The Vampa Museum Doylestown, PA January 2024

A new venue in Doylestown Pennsylvania has been attracting paranormal and vampire enthusiasts alike. The Vampa (Vampire/ Paranormal Museum) curated by Edmondo Crimi houses over 700 Vampire killing kits, all types of macabre furniture and art and eerie sculptures depicting vampires and showcasing the battle between good and evil.

In 2022 I had approached Ed about being a sponsor for my tv show but then quickly saw how he was opening this museum and how it would make an awesome episode of Eric Mintel Investigates. We kept seeing each other and I would always ask when are we going to collaborate but Ed, at the time, was traveling all over Europe buying and selling but eventually about a year later we saw each other at the gym and I asked him again and he said "we are ready!" The series we are doing is called "Paranormal Pickers!" created by Ed, it follows his journey into the world of antiquities and the world of haunted objects. At the start of this series we began with Ed getting a call to pick up a doll that the homeowners did not want anymore and thought the doll would be a great addition tot he museum. The doll was originally from the Robert Thomas Estate. Robert Thomas created the Farmers Almanac. On this day, Ed, myself, my cameraman Tom Brunt and JD

Mullane reporter for USA Today traveled to
the location where this mysterious doll was
housed. The homeowners were not home but
we were told by Ed's friend Nick that it was in
a storage shed out side on the grounds
somewhere. We arrived to find the shed in a
back part of the property way away from the
house. Robbie, Ed's worker and truck driver,
had a set of keys to open the shed with. As we
opened the door we were startled to find that
the shed was very long and went back about

75 feet. As we looked around for the doll we suddenly found a piece of furniture draped with cloth and as Ed took off the cloth, the doll was revealed. The doll was absolutely weird, it had nails protruding out of it, it had a skull in its hand and a wood like face behind it. One of the creepiest things Ed had ever seen and all of us had ever seen. Ed called Nick to tell him that it was definitely not a kids toy! It had a lot of dark energy around it. Ed reluctantly agreed to take it for the museum and had Robbie put it in the truck. Ed was visibly shaken and wanted to go to church to wash off the evil he felt from this doll. As we headed to the church we got a frantic call from Robbie saying the truck broke down! We all looked at each other and said "He has the doll!" with that Robbie was going to try and get it started which he eventually did and we headed to the church. Ed, after saying some

blessings for us and the community, started to feel a little better. This would not be the first time we would encounter strange energy coming from an object.

Later that night the team converged onto the Vampa museum property where we would conduct a night investigation. Dominic arrived and we also invited Psychic medium

Julie Kraus on this one as well. Julie's powers of energy and healing were definitely needed on this case. Before we started, Julie Saged the team and protected us from harm.

We knocked on the barn door and Ed answered. Immediately Dominic felt strong energy coming from the upstairs corner of the barn. This was an area that earlier in the day I had something fall near me while I was shooting some b roll. Keep in mind I said nothing to Dominic or Julie about any activity going on there. Julie was getting hits right away as well and told Ed something that made Ed's jaw drop to which he said he could not even talk about it with anyone. With that realization that something beyond us was going on here we decided to head upstairs and check it out. As soon as we got upstairs the temperature dropped and we were freezing. We went lights out and again all that we were using was our night vision camera. Oddly enough the magnetometer was reading zero on this investigation so far. We gathered into the back of the barn where Dominic and

Julie were feeling strong energy and as we talked Julie mentioned that she felt a light or chandelier fell down and hit someone. Dominic in another part of the barn and not in earshot of Julie said "Did a chandelier fall on someone?" Ed said that a chandelier fell on him a while ago and hit him on the top of his head. Julie said she was glad he was okay. As she said that we all heard what sounded like a kazoo sound coming from the area we were standing in. Dominic said he had heard that sound earlier but over in the museum when I was interviewing Julie. With the realization that something was in the barn with us, we cautiously looked around to see where the sound was coming from. We didn't hear it again but did hear slight knocks and footsteps. Ed's workers have been hearing voices in the barn early in the morning. So frightened that they are upset and threatening to quit.

We decided to wrap up the investigation and Julie once again Saged us for protection as we left the Vampa that night. Two weeks later I wanted to shoot some more footage of when Dominic said he heard that sound we heard in the barn coming from the Doll room in the museum. On this night, it was just me, Dominic and Ed who opened up for us late.

As is usually the case, I do a half shot of Dominic explaining activity he felt in an area.

This time he was positioned in front of the Doll room and as he was explaining what he heard and in his words sounded like batteries dying from a voice box (the dolls do not have

batteries or voice boxes) as soon as he said "batteries dying" we all heard a voice coming from behind Dominic and, from what we believe, the 5 foot Burmese doll. A doll with a spine tingling stare that also has real hair. Dominic felt an energy reach out and try to grab him! He was beyond shaken and so was Ed! I was the only calm one there that night. We captured the voice or growl or whatever it was on video. This is our latest release you can now watch parts 1 and 2 now available on our You Tube channel at Eric Mintel Investigates. The series we will do for the Vampa museum will deal with various haunted objects, the people Ed is involved with and what otherworldly activity we encounter.

Authors note:

Currently we are working on several video investigations and will have a companion book to go along with this one shortly. In the meantime I hope you will head over to our You Tube Channel and like and subscribe to Eric Mintel Investigates and check out the over 100 videos we have with investigations covering Ghosts to Bigfoot to UFO's to Dogman and many more yet to be discovered. The evidence is clear and to quote my good friend Paul Petersen Jr, "At the end of the day people are seeing something!"

Eric Mintel
May 2024
Bucks County, PA

Eric Mintel can be reached at emqjazz@gmail.com for any reports you may have. Thank you so much for purchasing this book!

Acknowledgments

To my beautiful Sherry who always believes in me and makes me always want to do and be better. I love you. My daughter Tess. I love you beyond words. Dominic Sattele who has joined me on many an investigation and always approaches each case with energy and enthusiasm. I couldn't do it without you. Julie Kraus for your enthusiasm and energy and availability to join us on some cases. Scott Chrysler our fearless camera man on the Beast of Bray Road Investigation who never flinched even when we heard those blood curdling howls. Tom Brunt our Bucks County cameraman who has followed and captured each investigation even in some spine tingling moments! Ed Crimi for working with me on the new Paranormal Pickers series of which we are having a blast! And lastly I want to sincerely thank Ellen Collins for not only her friendship, vision and enthusiasm for what we do at Eric Mintel Investigates but making the Beast of Bray Road Investigations possible to bring to you. Thank you!

And to you reading this book, I hope you find the stories and cases both compelling and entertaining. Everything you read actually happened.

For more videos please like and subscribe to the Eric Mintel Investigates You Tube Channel. Find us on Facebook and Instagram at Eric Mintel Investigates.

125

Made in the USA
Middletown, DE
21 July 2024

57794165R00070